HUMPTY DUMPTY

DANIEL KIRK

G. P. Putnam's Sons • New York

Special thanks to Jerry Fried for his generous
technical help in time of need.

Copyright © 2000 by Daniel Kirk
All rights reserved. This book, or parts thereof, may not be reproduced
in any form without permission in writing from the publisher.
G. P. PUTNAM'S SONS,
a division of Penguin Putnam Books for Young Readers,
345 Hudson Street, New York, NY 10014.
G. P. Putnam's Sons, Reg. U.S. Pat. & Tm. Off. Published simultaneously in Canada.
Printed in Hong Kong by South China Printing Co. (1988) Ltd.
Book designed by Semadar Megged. Text set in Bradlo Sans.
The art was done in oil paint on illustration board, with magazine clippings,
color photocopies and computer print-outs for the collage elements.
Library of Congress Cataloging-in-Publication Data
Kirk, Daniel. Humpty Dumpty / Daniel Kirk. p. cm.
Summary: While watching young King Moe's birthday parade, Humpty Dumpty falls
and breaks, but the King is able to put him back together.
ISBN 0-399-23332-6
[1. Eggs—Fiction. 2. Kings, queens, rulers, etc.—Fiction. 3. Parades—Fiction.
4. Birthdays—Fiction. 5. Stories in rhyme.] I. Title. PZ8.3.K6553 Ht 2000 [E]—dc21 99-046746
1 3 5 7 9 10 8 6 4 2
First Impression

For Julia,
who puts all the pieces
together again.

Humpty Dumpty stared at the wall,
for sitting at home was no fun at all.
He squirmed on the sofa and
wiggled his leg.
You can't be too careful
when you are an egg!

"There's nothing to do,"
Humpty said with a frown.
"It's not fair you won't let me
go into town.
Today's the big birthday parade
for King Moe.
All my friends will be there—
won't you please let me go?"
"Well all right," said his mom,
"but be careful, OK?
I don't want my egg getting
scrambled today!"

Young Humpty ran, not too fast, not too slow,
but as quickly as chubby egg boys ever go.
He raced to the town
where King Moe's castle stood.
This birthday parade was going to be good!

All the King's horses and all the King's men
were waiting for King Moe's parade to begin.
But where was the King?
He was under his bed,
with his puzzles and toys.
"GO AWAY!" King Moe said.
"I can't ride a horse, and the coach is too high.
If I should fall off, I would probably die!
I'm scared of the clowns, and I hate a parade.
I'd rather stay home by myself, I'm afraid!"

"You're scared of your shadow,"
King Moe's mother cried.
"Whenever people come visit, you hide.
You're so terribly shy,
you can't make a friend.
Come on, have some fun.
That's what I'd recommend!"

At the curb the crowd gathered.
Humpty Dumpty was ready
to enjoy the parade with his pals,
Ben and Teddy.
Trumpets blared, bells rang out
from the top of the steeple
as the kids tried to see
past the masses of people.

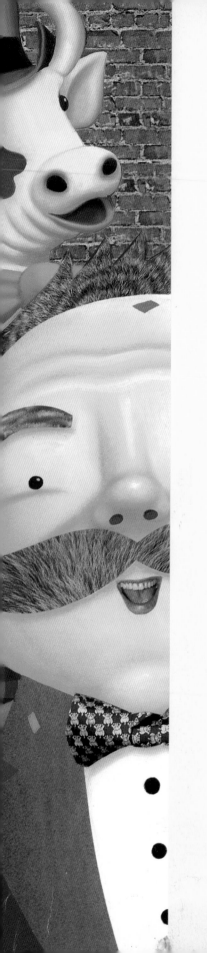

"Help me up," pleaded Humpty,
"from down here I can't see!"
He climbed on the backs
of his friends—one, two, three.
To their shoulders he climbed,
with a huff and a puff,
but though taller, he still
wasn't quite tall enough.
"The lamp post!" he cried,
as he twisted a shoe.
"From up there I'd get
a spectacular view!"

The jugglers were juggling,
baton twirlers twirled;
but King Moe, the most
timid boy in the world,
looked pale as he groaned,
"It's a curse being King!
I can't find a seatbelt
to wear in this thing!"

A policeman saw Humpty
and yelled, "COME ON DOWN!
WE DON'T ALLOW CLIMBING
ON POLES IN THIS TOWN!"
Humpty slid down the lamp post.
"That's all right," he said,
"I think I'll climb up
on that brick wall instead!"

Moe waved from the window.
The townspeople cheered.
At the top of the wall,
Humpty Dumpty appeared.
Moe hollered, "Look, Mother,
up on the wall!
If that egg isn't careful,
he's going to fall!"

"Happy birthday, King Moe!"
Humpty started to yell.
It was then that the egg
lost his footing and fell.
He flipped through the air,
and then in a flash,
tore straight through
the roof of the coach
with a crash!

All the King's horses
and all the King's men
couldn't put Humpty together again.
Moe picked up some shell
and started to cry.
Then his mom whispered,
"Dear, why don't **you** give a try?
It's just like a puzzle," she said with a wink.
The King set to work. "I can do it, I think!"

Moe patched up the egg.
Humpty looked good as new,
except for his nose,
and a bandage or two.
"You're clever," said Humpty.
"You're brave," said the King.
"Though fragile and round,
you will try anything!"
"How you fixed me,"
said Humpty, "I don't
have a clue.
I wish I were thoughtful
and patient, like you!

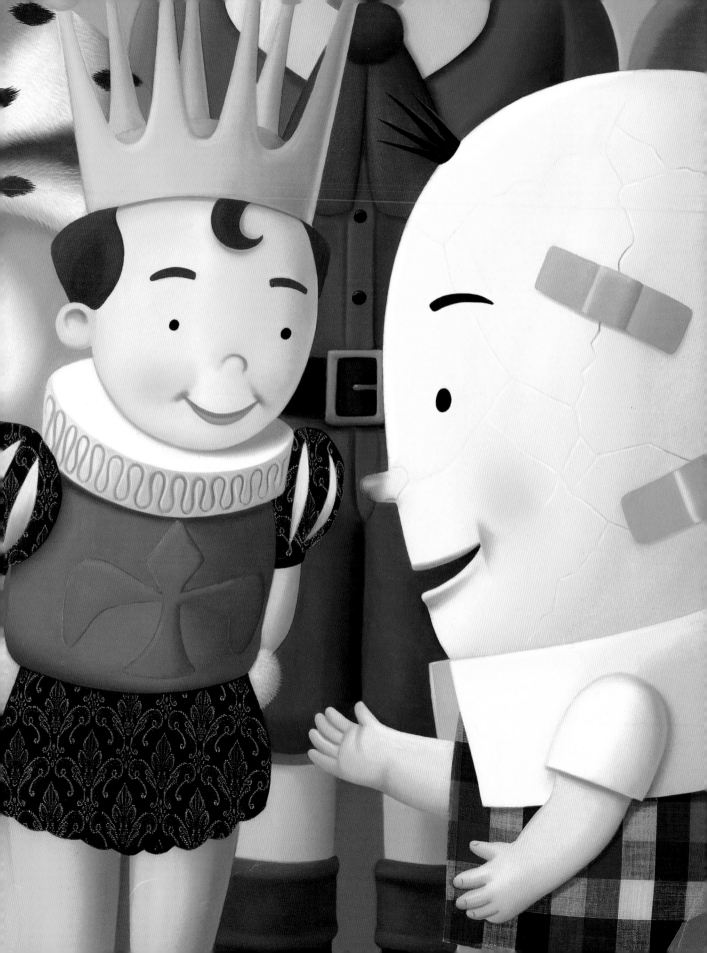

"I'm an egg, you're a King,
but what do you say—
would you like to come over
to my house and play?"
"May I go?" pleaded Moe.
"Oh, Mother, say yes!"
"Absolutely," she smiled,
"Humpty, what's your address?"
The boys climbed on top
of the carriage to ride.
"HOORAY! It's my best birthday
EVER!" Moe cried.

To the house of the egg,
the parade made its way;
and King Moe and Humpty
are friends to this day.